A Click Clack Book

D1111984

Pool Party!

By Doreen Cronin

Illustrated by Betsy Lewin

Ready-to-Read

Simon Spotlight

New York London Toronto Sydney New Delhi

For Jamie and Claire
—D. C.

For Clara
—B. L.

SIMON SPOTLIGHT
An imprint of Simon & Schuster Children's Publishing Division
1230 Avenue of the Americas, New York, New York 10020
This Simon Spotlight edition May 2020
Text copyright © 2020 by Doreen Cronin
Illustrations copyright © 2020 by Betsy Lewin
All rights reserved, including the right of reproduction in whole or in part in any form.
SIMON SPOTLIGHT, READY-TO-READ, and colophon are registered trademarks of Simon & Schuster, Inc.
For information about special discounts for bulk purchases, please contact Simon & Schuster
Special Sales at 1-866-506-1949 or business@simonandschuster.com.
Manufactured in the United States of America 0320 LAK
10 9 8 7 6 5 4 3 2 1
Library of Congress Cataloging-in-Publication Data
Names: Cronin, Doreen, author. | Lewin, Betsy, illustrator.
Title: Pool party! / by Doreen Cronin ; illustrated by Betsy Lewin.
Description: New York : Simon Spotlight, 2020. | Series: Ready to read.
Level 2: A click clack book | Audience: Ages 5 - 7 | Summary: On a hot summer day,
Farmer Brown and the animals enjoy getting cool in the pool.
Identifiers: LCCN 2019041526 | ISBN 9781534454170 (pbk) |
ISBN 9781534454187 (hc) | ISBN 9781534454194 (eBook)
Subjects: CYAC: Domestic animals—Fiction. | Swimming pools—Fiction. |
Counting. | Humorous stories.
Classification: LCC PZ7.C88135 Po 2020 | DDC [E]—dc23
LC record available at https://lccn.loc.gov/2019041526

It is a summer day.
The animals are very hot.
Farmer Brown does not have a pool.
Farmer Brown has a pond.

Farmer Brown calls his brother, Bob.
Bob does not have a pond.
Bob has a pool.

"Come on over!" says Bob.

Bob gives everyone
sunscreen.

Bob gives everyone a
pair of goggles.

Bob gives everyone a towel.

Now everyone is ready to get cool
in the pool!

Duck is an excellent swimmer.
He is the first one in the pool.

Splash!

The water feels good.
One duck swims in the pool.

Farmer Brown and Bob
are excellent swimmers.
They jump in the pool together.

"Hooray!" says
Farmer Brown.
Splash!

"Hooray!" says
his brother, Bob.
Splash!

The water feels good.
Two brothers and one duck
are cool in the pool.

The chickens are excellent divers.
They dive off the diving board.

"Cluck! Cluck! Cluck!"

Splash!

Splash!

Splash!

The water feels good.
Three chickens, two brothers,
and one duck are loud in the pool.

The pigs wade into the pool.
They know the backstroke.
"Oink! Oink! Oink! Oink!"
say the pigs.

Splash!

Splash!

Splash! Splash!

The water feels good.
Four pigs, three chickens,
two brothers, and one duck
are a little crowded in the pool!

The cows do not like to be splashed.
They do not want to go in the pool.

"We will not splash," says Farmer Brown.

"Duck will not splash," says Bob.

"The chickens will not splash," says Farmer Brown.

"The pigs will not splash," says Bob.

The cows still do not want
to go in the pool.

It is too loud for the cows.
It is too crowded for the cows.

One duck gets out of the pool.
Two brothers get out of the pool.

Three chickens get out of the pool.
Four pigs get out of the pool.

There is no splashing
in the pool now.

It is not loud in the pool now.
It is not crowded in the pool now.

The cows are ready for the pool.

Five cows jump off the diving board.

There is splashing in the pool now.

Five cows float in the pool!

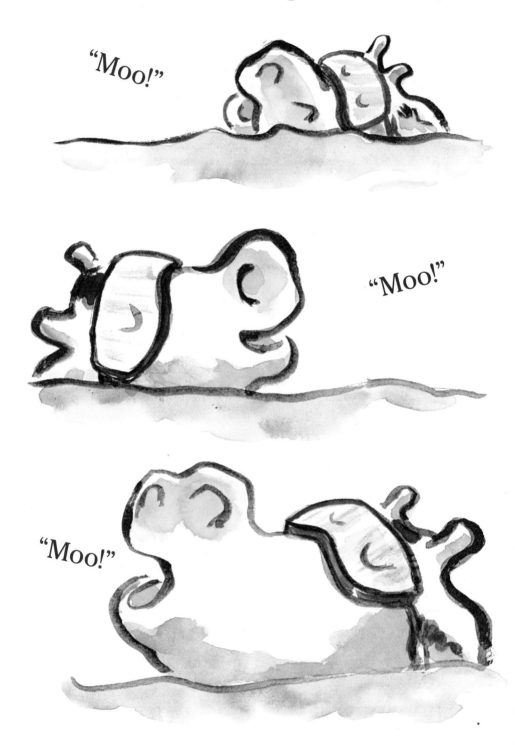

"Moo!"

"Moo!"

It is loud in the pool now.

Five cows try to do the backstroke
in the pool.
It is too crowded for five cows
to do the backstroke in the pool.

Four pigs, three chickens,
two brothers, and one duck
are feeling hot out of the pool.

The cows make room for one duck.

The cows make room
for two brothers.

The cows make room
for three chickens.

The cows make room for four pigs.

It is very splashy in the pool now.
It is very loud in the pool now.
It is very crowded in the pool now.

It is fun for everyone to be cool
in the pool now!